Franklin's Halloween

ISBN 0-590-69330-1

Published by Scholastic Inc., 555 Broadway, New York, NY 10012,
by arrangement with Kids Can Press Ltd.
Interior illustrations prepared with the assistance of Muriel Hughes Wood.

12 11 10 9 8 7 6 5 4 3 2 1 6 7 8 9/9

Printed in the U.S.A. 09

First Scholastic printing, September 1996

Franklin's Halloween

Paulette Bourgeois
Brenda Clark

SCHOLASTIC INC.
New York Toronto London Auckland Sydney

FRANKLIN could count by twos and tie his shoes. He knew the days of the week, the months of the year, and the holidays in every season. Today was October 31. It was Halloween! Franklin could hardly wait for tonight's costume party. Everyone would be there.

HALLOWEEN
PARTY
Costume
Contest

Franklin and his friends had talked about the party for weeks. There would be games, prizes, and even a parade. Best of all, there would be a haunted house.

"I think there'll be bats and spiders," said Franklin.

"And skeletons," added Beaver.

Rabbit shivered. "My sister says she saw a real ghost in there last year."

"That's silly, Rabbit," said Beaver. "There are no *real* ghosts."

All of Franklin's friends were excited because of the costume contest.

Franklin wasn't sure what he was going to wear. He'd tried on everything in his dress-up trunk, but nothing seemed quite right.

Beaver and Goose were keeping their costumes secret.

"Try to find us at the party," they giggled.

Fox was also mysterious about what he was going to be.

"Look for something gruesome," he said.

That gave Franklin an idea. He would be something creepy.

It took Franklin more than an hour to make his costume.

As soon as it was done, he sneaked up behind his father and tapped him on the shoulder.

"Trick or treat," said Franklin.

"Ahhhh!" gasped his father. "Who are you?"

In his deepest, spookiest voice, Franklin answered, "It's me. Franklinstein!"

On the way to town, Franklin tried to guess who was inside each costume.

"At least I don't have to worry about finding Bear," said Franklin. "He's always a ghost."

By the time Franklin and his parents arrived, the party had started.

Franklin spotted a ghost at the apple-bobbing and hurried toward him. "Hello, Bear," Franklin said.

"Whooo!" answered the ghost.

"That's good, Bear," said Franklin. "You sound really scary."

Franklin bobbed for an apple. Then he ran to the pumpkin toss. It was his favorite game because he always won a treat.

Franklin's bag was almost full by the time the judges announced the costume contest. While everyone lined up for the parade, Franklin tried to find more of his friends. He thought he recognized Beaver and Goose. But where was Fox?

They marched around the building twice.

Franklin made horrible monster sounds and shuffled with stiff, straight legs. He won a prize for being the best green monster.

There was only one more thing to do – go into the haunted house.

"You first," said Beaver, pushing Franklin toward the door.

It creaked open. A skeleton rattled. Chains clanged. There were moans. Franklin stepped on something crunchy.

Suddenly, a big hairy hand reached out of the darkness.

Franklin's heart beat hard and fast. But before he could scream, a light was flicked on.

"Trick or treat!" shouted Mr. Mole.

Franklin looked around nervously. Then he laughed. The hairy hand was only Mr. Mole's mop.

"Here's a treat for braving the haunted house," said Mr. Mole. "A ghost came before you. He got so scared he flew away."

"But Bear can't fly," said Franklin.

"It wasn't Bear," explained Mr. Mole. "Bear is home sick with a nasty cold."

Franklin shuddered. "If Bear wasn't the ghost, then who was?"

He ran back to his friends, who were waiting in line for the haunted house.

"Was it that scary?" asked Fox. "You look like you've seen a ghost."

"Maybe I did," said Franklin. He told them what Mr. Mole had said.

"You mean that Bear was never here?" asked Beaver.

Franklin shook his head.

The ghost flew over them. It swooped low and called, "Whooo!"

Rabbit twitched. "So what is white, says 'Whooo,' and flies?"

"A real ghost," answered Goose. "Run!"

Franklin was about to follow when he saw a feather floating down.

"Stop!" he shouted. "I think I know *whooo* the ghost is."

Franklin showed them the feather. "Look. It must be Mr. Owl."

Even Rabbit giggled when he realized the trick their teacher had played.

By the end of the party, everyone's bag was full.

"Poor Bear," said Raccoon. "No treats for him."

"We could share our treats with Bear," suggested Franklin.

All the friends agreed. They each put some treats into a bag. Then they walked to Bear's house and left the bag on the doorstep.

"Trick *and* treat!" they called.

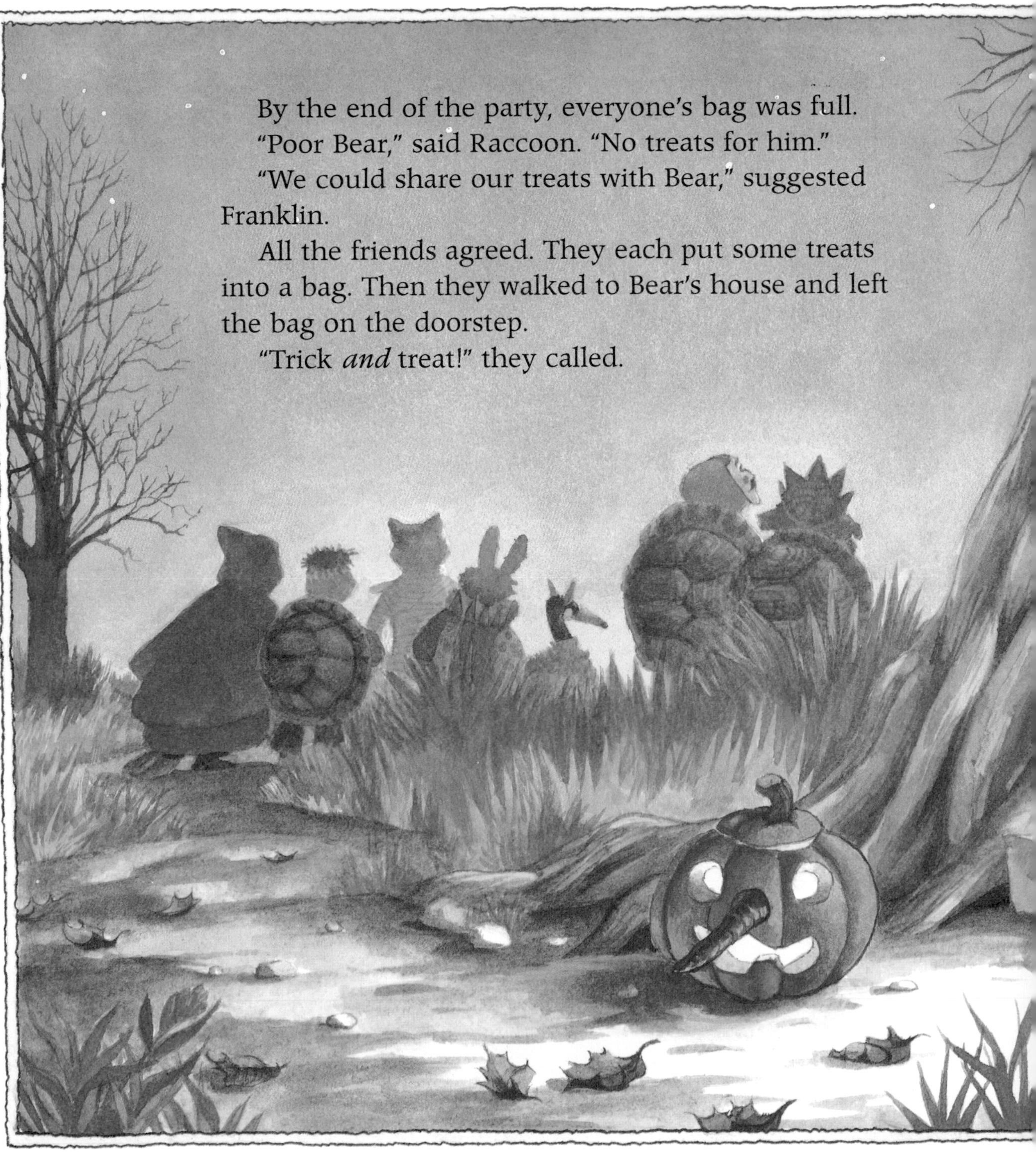

On the way home, Franklin looked into his treat bag.

"Goodness!" said his mother. "You have enough there to last until next Halloween."

"Maybe," said Franklin, sampling a few. But secretly he hoped the treats would last until the end of the week.